ELECTION DAY

HEATHER C. HUDAK

www.av2books.com

MEDIA ENHANCED BOOKS

AV²
BY WEIGL™

ADDED VALUE • AUDIO VISUAL

Go to **www.av2books.com**, and enter this book's unique code.

BOOK CODE

P538697

AV² by Weigl brings you media enhanced books that support active learning.

AV² provides enriched content that supplements and complements this book. Weigl's AV² books strive to create inspired learning and engage young minds in a total learning experience.

Your AV² Media Enhanced books come alive with...

Audio
Listen to sections of the book read aloud.

Video
Watch informative video clips.

Embedded Weblinks
Gain additional information for research.

Try This!
Complete activities and hands-on experiments.

Key Words
Study vocabulary, and complete a matching word activity.

Quizzes
Test your knowledge.

Slide Show
View images and captions, and prepare a presentation.

... and much, much more!

Published by AV² by Weigl
350 5th Avenue, 59th Floor
New York, NY 10118
Web site: www.av2books.com   www.weigl.com

Library of Congress Control Number: 2012941021

ISBN 978-1-61913-863-6 (hardcover)

ISBN 978-1-61913-866-7 (softcover)

Printed in the United States of America in North Mankato, Minnesota

1 2 3 4 5 6 7 8 9 0 16 15 14 13 12

062012
WEP170512

Editor Heather Kissock   **Design** Terry Paulhus

Weigl acknowledges Getty Images as its primary image supplier for this book.

CONTENTS

What Is Election Day?

Election Day is the day after the first Monday in November each year. On this day, any of the states can hold an election. People vote in elections for leaders. These leaders are called public officials. Countries where people vote are called democracies.

⭐ Political conventions are held before an election. Presidential candidates are selected at these gatherings.

People running for **president** must be at least 35 years of age and citizens of the United States. They must also have lived in the country for at least 14 years. On Election Day, most Americans 18 years of age or older can vote. Every four years on Election Day, people vote for **electors**. They are representatives of the 50 states. Electors cast their votes for the president of the United States.

Special Events
THROUGHOUT THE YEAR

RAMADAN
THE EXACT DATES VARY FROM YEAR TO YEAR. IT IS ALWAYS THE NINTH MONTH OF THE MUSLIM CALENDAR.

JANUARY 1
NEW YEAR'S DAY

FEBRUARY (THIRD MONDAY)
PRESIDENTS' DAY

MARCH 17
ST. PATRICK'S DAY

SUNDAY IN MARCH OR APRIL
EASTER

MAY (LAST MONDAY)
MEMORIAL DAY

JUNE 14
FLAG DAY

JULY 4
INDEPENDENCE DAY

SEPTEMBER (FIRST MONDAY)
LABOR DAY

OCTOBER (SECOND MONDAY)
COLUMBUS DAY

NOVEMBER
ELECTION DAY

DECEMBER 25
CHRISTMAS DAY

Election History

The United States declared **independence** from Great Britain on July 4, 1776. Each state was given the power to make voting and election laws.

On January 7, 1789, the first presidential election took place. George Washington was the first president of the United States. John Adams became the first vice president.

✯ **George Washington is often called "The Father of Our Country" because of the role he played in making the United States an independent country.**

At first, only landowners were allowed to vote. By 1860, all men of European background over the age of 21 were allowed to vote. After the **American Civil War**, men of all **ethnic** backgrounds were able to vote. Then, in August of 1920, the 19ᵗʰ Amendment was passed, granting women the right to vote in federal elections. In 1965, the Voting Rights Act was passed. It outlawed practices like literacy tests that were used to keep people from voting.

Past and Present Elections

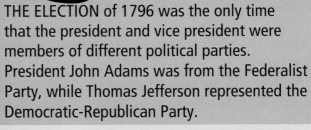

THE ELECTION of 1796 was the only time that the president and vice president were members of different political parties. President John Adams was from the Federalist Party, while Thomas Jefferson represented the Democratic-Republican Party.

IN 1971, the **Constitution** was amended to lower the voting age to 18. Prior to 1971, voters were required to be 21 years of age. The age was changed as a result of the Vietnam War. People felt that, if 18-year-olds could go to war, they could vote in elections.

IN 2008, Barack Obama became the first African American to be elected president. At midnight on election night in 2008, the **president-elect** made a speech to more than one million supporters in Chicago, Illinois, to celebrate this historic event.

The Election Process

Before Americans can vote, they must register with their district. To register, voters fill out a form that provides information about their identity. People can usually register by mail. In some places, people can register on the Internet.

Most Americans do not vote for the president. On Election Day, they vote for an elector, who will support the person they want to be president. This is called the popular vote. It is held in November.

⭐ As the election results come in, people gather to keep track of how each state voted.

The **Electoral College** votes for the president every four years in December. The college is made up of electors representing the 50 states and the District of Columbia. Their vote makes the popular vote official. The new president is declared on January 6 and is sworn into office on January 20, which is called Inauguration Day.

✯ **Following the Electoral College vote, the ballots are carried into Congress to be confirmed and the official winner declared.**

First-hand Account

"What is the use of being elected or re-elected unless you stand for something?"

—*Grover Cleveland, 1887, on refusing to change his position on tariffs*

Election Day

On Election Day, Americans vote at polls. Polls are usually in public buildings, such as schools, recreation centers, or firehouses. Not all districts use the same method of voting. Some use devices, such as voting machines or computers. Others have paper ballots.

⭐ The United States first began using electronic voting machines in 1964. Today, there are several types of voting machines, including those with touch screens.

Washington, DC is host to several inaugural balls, which celebrate the swearing in of the new president.

Once the polls have closed, poll workers count the ballots. Election officials tally votes around the state and around the nation. The president-elect is determined indirectly through the Electoral College. Presidential candidates are rewarded electoral votes for each state when they win the popular vote. Since 1964, there have been 538 electors in each presidential election based on the number of representatives and senators for each state.

Elections Around the World

ROMANIA

In Romania, the president is elected for a five-year term, not four as in the United States. The current president is Traian Basescu. He was elected in 2004 and reelected in 2009.

CHILE

In Chile, there are two elections for president for a six-year term. The first election selects the top two candidates from the many running for office, followed by a run-off between the top two candidates.

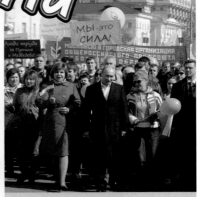

RUSSIA

In Russia, the president is elected every six years. Russian presidents cannot serve more than two terms in a row. Vladimir Putin, the current president, was elected in 2012. He is serving his third term.

Celebrating Today

Today, many people run for office. They must compete for support. Presidential candidates make television commercials. They tour the country and hold rallies. Large crowds of people in cities and towns gather at these rallies. Candidates give speeches to gain support from electors and voters.

⭐ Many people can vote at the same time, but each person has a special location. This keeps each person's vote private.

Television, radio, newspapers, and the Internet bring election news to people across the United States and around the world. This helps people learn about candidates and what they believe in.

In America, if voters do not like the proposed candidates for president, they can write in their own preferred person for the job.

★ Candidates prepare campaign signs to increase their visibility prior to an election.

Election Day in the United States

Americans have the right and the privilege to vote. It is important to be part of the process. Voting allows people to voice their opinions. There are many voting systems. Here are just a few of the systems used across the United States.

Oregon

Nevada

NEVADA
People in Nevada use electronic touch-screen machines to cast their vote. Registered voters are given a card that contains their personal information. They insert their card in the machine and begin selecting their candidates.

OREGON
In Oregon, ballots are mailed to voters. People must first register as voters. When it is time to vote, ballots are mailed to everyone on the voters list. Voters can mail their ballot in or deposit it at an official ballot dropsite.

Hawai'i

0   970 Miles

Alaska

0   1,278 Miles

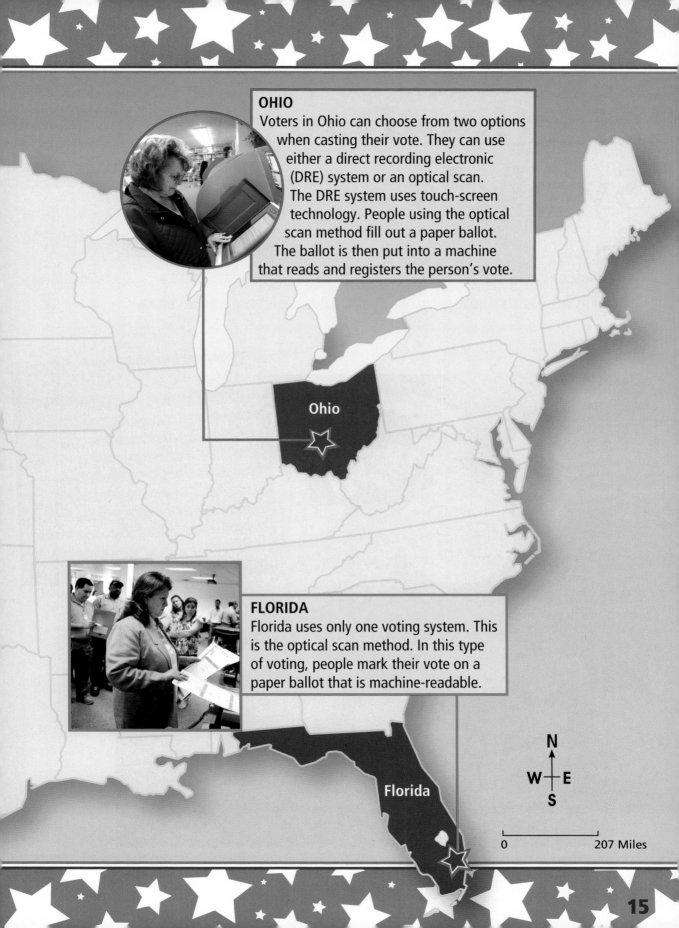

OHIO

Voters in Ohio can choose from two options when casting their vote. They can use either a direct recording electronic (DRE) system or an optical scan. The DRE system uses touch-screen technology. People using the optical scan method fill out a paper ballot. The ballot is then put into a machine that reads and registers the person's vote.

Ohio

FLORIDA

Florida uses only one voting system. This is the optical scan method. In this type of voting, people mark their vote on a paper ballot that is machine-readable.

Florida

N
W E
S

0   207 Miles

Election Day Symbols

Election Day is an important time in the United States. Each election is a part of America's history. There are many symbols that are part of Election Day history and events.

CAMPAIGN BUTTONS

The first political buttons were used at the inauguration of George Washington. The first presidential campaign button was used in 1896. Since then, all candidates have created buttons to help convince people to vote for them. Some buttons just encourage people to vote without mentioning the candidates.

THE CONSTITUTION

In 1787, the **Founding Fathers** wrote the Constitution of the United States of America. The Constitution is made up of laws. It also tells how the government should work. The Constitution describes how elections are held and how states get electoral votes. The electoral votes decide who becomes president.

THE OATH OF OFFICE

Every public official must say an oath of office. The oath is a promise to uphold the Constitution. The president-elect must take the oath at noon on January 20 of the year the term begins. The president-elect makes the promise in front of thousands of Americans.

A Song to Remember

"This Land Is Your Land" is a song that encourages Americans to take pride and ownership in their country. It was written by Woody Guthrie in 1940.

As I was walking
a ribbon of highway
I saw above me
an endless skyway
I saw below me
a golden valley
This land was made
for you and me

This land is your land
This land is my land
From California,
to the New York
Island
From the redwood
forest
to the gulf stream
waters
This land was made
for you and me.

-Woody Guthrie

Write Your Own Song

Songwriting is a fun way to express thoughts and ideas. Get creative, and write your own song.

Listen to a song that you like, and pay attention to the words. Which words rhyme? How many verses are there? How many lines are in each verse? How many times is the chorus sung?

Start brainstorming ideas. What do you want your song to be about? Choose an event, idea, person, or feeling you would like to write about.

Write the verses. Songs usually have three or four verses. Each one will be different but should relate to the chorus.

Think of a tune for your song. Some songwriters like to write the tune before the words. Others will write them at the same time.

Write the chorus to your song. The chorus is the main idea of the song. It connects the verses together.

Many songwriters work with other people to create songs. Try working with a classmate or friend to think of a tune or words for your song.

Have a Lunch Menu Election

To see how an election works, here is an election you can conduct in a classroom.

Shoe Box

Markers

Posterboard

6 Easy Steps to Lunch Menu Election

1 Form four groups of students.

2 Each group should select a food they want on the menu for a main dish at lunch. To avoid duplication of items, have the group write their selection on poster board so that other groups pick something different.

3 Have each group decorate their poster board to publicize their choices.

4 Have a member of each group "campaign" by giving a speech about their selection.

5 Have one group create ballots, a second group make a ballot box, a third group conduct the election, and the fourth group count the votes.

6 Declare a winner!

Make an Election Day Banana Split

Ingredients

2 scoops of vanilla
ice cream
1 ripe banana

cherries
blueberries
blue and red sprinkles

Equipment

ice cream scoop,
oval deep dish or
banana boat

Directions

1. Ask an adult to slice the banana in half lengthwise. Place at bottom of dish.
2. Place 2 scoops of vanilla side by side on top of the banana.
3. Sprinkle washed cherries and blueberries around the dish.
4. Top the scoops of ice cream with blue and red sprinkles, and serve.

Test Your Knowledge!

1 When was the Constitution written?

2 What are electors?

3 Who was allowed to vote in the first election?

4 When is the president-elect sworn into office?

5 When were all women allowed to vote in the United States?

Key Words

American Civil War: military conflict between the northern and southern states from 1861 to 1865

Congress: the national government body of the United States

constitution: a written document containing the basic laws of a nation

Electoral College: the number of electors for each presidential election is based on the number of state representatives for each state.

electors: delegates from each state

ethnic: having to do with a group of people with distinct cultural traits

Founding Fathers: members of the group that wrote the Constitution

independence: having the ability to support oneself

president: the leader of the United States government

president-elect: a person who has been elected to be the next president

Index

Log on to www.av2books.com

AV² by Weigl brings you media enhanced books that support active learning. Go to www.av2books.com, and enter the special code found on page 2 of this book. You will gain access to enriched and enhanced content that supplements and complements this book. Content includes video, audio, weblinks, quizzes, a slide show, and activities.

Audio
Listen to sections of the book read aloud.

Video
Watch informative video clips.

Embedded Weblinks
Gain additional information for research.

Try This!
Complete activities and hands-on experiments.

WHAT'S ONLINE?

 Try This!

Pages 8-9 Write a biography about an important person.

Pages 10-11 Describe the features and special events of a similar celebration around the world.

Pages 14-15 Complete a mapping activity about Election Day celebrations.

Pages 16-17 Try this activity about important holiday symbols.

Pages 20-21 Play an interactive activity.

 Embedded Weblinks

Pages 6-7 Find out more about the history of Election Day.

Pages 10-11 Learn more about similar celebrations around the world.

Pages 16-17 Find information about important holiday symbols.

Pages 18-19 Link to more information about Election Day.

Pages 20-21 Check out more holiday craft ideas.

 Video

Pages 4-5 Watch a video about Election Day

Pages 12-13 Check out a video about how people celebrate Election Day

EXTRA FEATURES

Audio
Listen to sections of the book read aloud.

Key Words
Study vocabulary, and complete a matching word activity.

Slide Show
View images and captions, and prepare a presentation.

Quizzes
Test your knowledge.

AV² was built to bridge the gap between print and digital. We encourage you to tell us what you like and what you want to see in the future.
Sign up to be an AV² Ambassador at www.av2books.com/ambassador.